Motorcycles for Kids

A Children's Picture Book About Motorcycles

A Great Simple Picture Book for Kids to Learn about Different Motorcycles

Melissa Ackerman

PUBLISHED BY:

Melissa Ackerman

Copyright © 2016

All rights reserved.

No part of this publication may be copied, reproduced in any format, by any means, electronic or otherwise, without prior consent from the copyright owner and publisher of this book.

Disclaimer

The information contained in this book is for general information purposes only. The information is provided by the authors and while we endeavor to keep the information up to date and correct, we make no representations or warranties of any kind, express or implied, about the completeness, accuracy, reliability, suitability or availability with respect to the book or the information, products, services, or related graphics contained in the book for any purpose. Any reliance you place on such information is therefore strictly at your own risk.

Other amazing picture books by Melissa Ackerman for young kids to enjoy

Butterflies for Kids

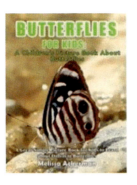

Spiders for Kids

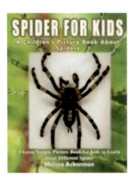

Animals in Africa

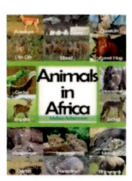

TABLE OF CONTENTS

APRILIA RS250 11

APRILIA RSV4 FACTORY 12

APRILIA TUONO 13

ARIAL SQUARE 4 14

BMW HP4 15

BMW R100S 16

BMW R1200GS 17

BMW R1200RT 18

BMW R32 19

BMW R69S 20

BMW S1000RR 21

BRAMMO EMPULSE R 22

BRITTEN V1000 23

BROUGH SUPERIOR SS 100 24

BSA BANTAM 25

BSA GOLD STAR 26

BSA ROCKET/ TRIUMPH TRIDENT 27

BUELL XB12R 28

CONFEDERATE WRAITH	29
DUCATI 1098	30
DUCATI 900SS	31
DUCATI 916	32
DUCATI 999R	33
DUCATI DESMOSEDICI RR	34
DUCATI MULTISTRADA	35
DUCATI SCRAMBLER	36
DUCATI SUPERMONO	37
HARLEY DAVIDSON LOW RIDER	38
HARLEY DAVIDSON ROAD KING	39
HARLEY DAVIDSON SOFTAIL	40
HONDA 400 FOUR	41
HONDA AFRICA TWIN	42
HONDA CB750	43
HONDA CBR1100XX SUPER BLACKBIRD	44
HONDA CBR900RR	45
HONDA CR500	46
HONDA CT90	47

HONDA MOTOCOMPO	48
HONDA NR	49
HONDA NX650 DOMINATOR	50
HONDA PAN EUROPEAN	51
HONDA RC30	52
HONDA RC51	53
HONDA RUNE	54
HONDA SUPER CUB	55
HONDA VFR 800	56
INDIAN CHIEF DARK HORSE	57
INDIAN CHIEF VINTAGE	58
INDIAN SCOUT	59
KAWASAKI ELIMINATOR	60
KAWASAKI NINJA H2	61
KAWASAKI VERSYS 650	62
KAWASAKI W800	63
KAWASAKI Z1	64
KAWASAKI ZX-10 TOMCAT	65
KAWASAKI ZZR600	66

KTM 1190 ADVENTURE	67
KTM 1190 RC8	68
KTM 950 ADVENTURE	69
LAVERDA JOTA	70
METISSE DESERT RACER	71
MOTO GUZZI LE MANS	72
MOTO GUZZI V7 RACER	73
MOTO GUZZI V8	74
MTT Y2K TURBINE MOTORCYCLE	75
NORTON 961 COMMANDO	76
NORTON COMMANDO	77
NORTON JUBILEE	78
NORTON MANX	79
ROYAL ENFIELD CONTINENTAL GT	80
SAIETTA R	81
SUZUKI 600 BANDIT	82
SUZUKI BIPLANE	83
SUZUKI BOULEVARD C50	84
SUZUKI BOULEVARD M50	85

SUZUKI GSX-R 750	86
SUZUKI HAYABUSA	87
SUZUKI INTRUDER	88
SUZUKI RG500 GAMMA	89
SUZUKI SV650	90
SUZUKI V STORM 650	91
TRIUMPH BONNEVILLE	92
TRIUMPH MODEL H	93
TRIUMPH SPEED TRIPLE	94
TRIUMPH THRUXTON	95
TRIUMPH TIGER 900	96
TRIUMPH X75 HURRICANE	98
VELOCETTE VENOM	99
VINCENT BLACK SHADOW	100
YAMAHA FS1-E	101
YAMAHA FZR600	102
YAMAHA GTS 1000	103
YAMAHA RD350LC	104
YAMAHA ROAD STAR	105

YAMAHA SDR 200 106

YAMAHA THUNDERCAT 107

YAMAHA VIRAGO 535 108

YAMAHA XT500 109

YAMAHA YZF R1 110

YAMAHA YZF-R7 111

Aprilia RS250

The Aprilia RS250 is a sport bike, or a motorcycle the features great speed and acceleration, and is typically used in races. It was produced by Aprilia—an Italian motorcycle manufacturer—from 1995 to 2002. It was also specifically designed to resemble Aprilia's GP250 bike in line with their celebration of being the champion in the 1994 and 1995 Grand Prix motorcycle racing season. The Aprilia RS250 boasts two mufflers, 19.5 liter fuel capacity, an entirely fiberglass body and a no-scratch windscreen.

Aprilia RSV4 Factory

The Aprilia RSV4 Factory is another motorcycle from Aprilia. It is considered a super bike, or a high-performance motorcycle, with larger engine typically used in superbike racing. In comparison to its sister, the standard Aprilia RSV4, the Aprilia RSV4 Factory is way pricier but lighter in weight, making it easier to maneuver. At a quick glance there really is no distinguishable difference between the Factory and the standard RSV4. However, upon closer inspection, the Factory has the trademark gold front forks compared to the black forks fitted on the Standard RSV4. These front forks are the ones that connect the front wheel to the motorcycle's body.

Aprilia Tuono

The Aprilia Tuono is a naked motorcycle, or a general-purpose street motorcycle, that features an upright riding position. Street motorcycles are used on paved roads. It is manufactured since 2002 by Aprilia, an Italian motorcycle company. It has an 18-liter fuel capacity, 33 inch seat height and weighs 181 kilograms. The Aprilia Tuono also comes in six variants: April Tuono R Limited, RSV Tuono, RSV Tuono Factory, Tuono 1000 R, Tuono 100 R Factory and Tuono V4 APRC. All these variants, which almost look the same, only have some minor difference and varying engine performance.

Arial Square 4

The Ariel Square Four is a motorcycle built by Ariel Motorcycles, a British motorcycle manufacturer. It was produced from 1931 to 1959 and was designed by Edward Turner. Its name was derived from its engine design, called square four that features four cylinders arranged by twos on each side. It has about 23 liter fuel capacity and weighs around 193 kilograms. The Ariel Square Four is also available in four versions: 4F, 4G Mark I and Mark II.

BMW HP4

The BMW HP4 is a variant of the BMW S1000RR. It is considered one of the most powerful and effective superbikes on the market because of its capability to be used in all riding conditions. A super bike is a high performance sport bike that has a larger engine and is specifically designed for racing. In comparison to S1000RR, the HP4 is about 9kg lighter, faster, smoother, easier to drive and has fatter tire on the rear end. Furthermore, the HP4 has an overall length of 2.06 meters and a seat height of 0.82 meters. It also weighs around 169 kilograms and features a 17.5 liters fuel capacity.

BMW R100S

The R100S was a motorcycle built between 1976 and 1980 by BMW Motorrad, a unit of the German company BMW. It has a top speed of 120 miles per hour and a 24 liter fuel capacity. It also comes with a 32-inch seat height and a weight of 220 kilograms. It was available in different colors such as white, blue, red, metallic red, two tone red, black and silver. In 1977, an R100S won the Castrol Six Hour motorcycle race. The Castrol Six Hour race was a six-hour endurance race held in Australia from 1970 to 1987. And today, the R100S is considered one of the best motorcycles used in long distance travel.

BMW R1200GS

The BMW R1200GS is a German motorcycle produced by BMW Motorrad. It is a dual sport motorcycle, or a motorcycle that can be used off-road and can be registered and licensed for use on public roads. The R1200GS is a successful model and is really popular. In fact, as of 2012, the R1200GS was BMW's top-selling motorcycle and was even called "the most successful motorcycle in the last two-and-a-half decades" by Cycle World, a motorcycling magazine in the US. Additionally, it is also considered the model that created the adventure touring category of motorcycles. This particular category is for motorcycles that are especially designed for long range travel both on roads and off roads.

BMW R1200RT

The BMW R1200RT is a sport touring motorcycle from BMW Motorrad. A sport touring motorcycle is a motorcycle that combines the performance of a sport bike and the long-distance capabilities and comfort that a touring motorcycle can provide. It was launched in 2005 as a replacement for the R1150RT model. It features a 25 liter fuel capacity and an adjustable seat height from 0.82 to 0.84 meters. However, a low seat option from 0.78 to 0.80 meters seat height is also available. The R1200RT is a favored model of different institutions. In fact, factory built versions of R1200RT were made specifically for emergency services, like police use, paramedic use, blood transfusion, escort duty and fire services. In the United Kingdom, Ireland, California and Los Angeles, R1200RTs are remarkably popular in the police force.

BMW R32

The BMW R32 was a motorcycle produced by the German company BMW in 1923. It was the first motorcycle that the company built with a BMW name. It has a tubular steel frame and an engine that can produce 8.5 hp of power and a top speed of 59 mph. Additionally, the R32 also features a 14 liter fuel capacity. This motorcycle is 122 kilograms in weight, 2.1 meters overall length, 0.95 meters overall height and 0.80 meters overall width.

BMW R69S

The R69S was a motorcycle built in Munich, Germany by BMW Motorrad. Its production started in 1960 and ended in 1969 with a total of 11,317 units built. It had 109 miles per hour top speed, 17-liter fuel capacity, a length of 2.13 meters and a height of 0.98 meters. The R69S was equipped with a few luxurious touches including the Earles fork and a steering damper. The Earles fork is a patented design triangular fork that is specifically built for side car use. This particular fork also makes the front end of a motorcycle rise when braking hard. On the other hand, a steering damper is a device that inhibits the wobbling of the motorcycle when driven.

BMW S1000RR

The BMW S1000RR is a sport bike manufactured by BMW Motorrad from 2009 up to present. It was originally designed to compete in the 2009 Superbike World Championship; hence, only 1000 units were produced to meet the requirements of the competition. However, since 2010, the S1000RR is being mass-produced and is sold commercially. It is about 207.7 kilograms in weight, 2.06 meters in length, 0.83 meters in width and has a 0.82 meter seat height. It can also produce 179.2 hp of power and can carry 17.5 liters of fuel. The SR1000RR won its first race in the 2012 World Superbike competition at the British round in Donington Park.

Brammo Empulse R

The Brammo Empulse R is an electric motorcycle built by the American company Brammo, Inc. The deliveries of the first Empulse Rs happened in 2012. It can reach a top speed of 105 miles per hour and can run as far as 75 miles. It weighs around 200 kg and is available in colors like red, black and white. The Empulse R received a couple of awards from Playboy, an American men's lifestyle and entertainment magazine. These awards include: 2013 Motorcycle of the Year and 2013 Best Electric Motorcycle.

Britten V1000

This race motorcycle designed and hand built by Britten Motorcycle Company, a motorcycle manufacturer from Christchurch, New Zealand was produced from 1991 to 1998. There were only 10 Britten V1000s built in total, which are all now in collections and museums all over the world. The Britten V1000 features 188 miles per hour top speed and 24 liters fuel capacity. This particular motorcycle also delivers unbelievable performance that made it win several competitions like Battle of the Twins and New Zealand National Superbike Championship. The Britten V1000 also set a couple of world records including: World flying mile record (1000 cc and under), World standing start 1/4-mile (400 m) record (1000 cc and under), World standing start mile record (1000 cc and under) and World standing start kilometer record (1000 cc and under).

Brough Superior SS 100

This custom motorcycle built by George Brough was manufactured from 1924 to 1940. Every Brough Superior SS 100 or the "Rolls Royce of Motorcycles" as advertised by its manufacturer was designed to meet clients' specific requirements; like the shape of the handlebars as requested by customers. In 1925, there were about sixty-nine SS100s completed. The Brough Superior SS 100 won over 50 competitions in the early 1920s. This motorcycle has an 18 liter fuel capacity and a varying top speed from 100 – 130.6 miles per hour.

BSA Bantam

The BSA Bantam is a lightweight motorcycle manufactured by the British company Birmingham Small Arms Company (BSA). It was built from 1948 to 1971 with an estimated 250,000 to half a million units produced. It features a teardrop-shaped tank that can hold 8.0, 8.6, or 9.1 liters of fuel depending on the model. The Bantam also comes in different variants, with the first one being the D1 (like the image above). The D1 has a look that almost resembles a bicycle: with one cushioned seat for the driver and a metal frame for the passenger.

BSA Gold Star

The BSA Gold Star is another motorcycle from Birmingham Small Arms Company. It was manufactured from 1938 to 1963. This motorcycle was considered one of the fastest bikes of the 1950s. The history of this motorcycle started in 1937 when Wal Handley lapped the Brooklands circuit at over 100 mph using a BSA Empire Star. Because of this, the Empire Star was awarded one of the traditional Gold Star pins. This award inspired the BSA to produce the BSA Gold Star. This particular motorcycle model features clip-on handlebars, chrome plated fuel tank with 18-liter capacity, swept-back exhaust and .77 meters seat height.

BSA Rocket/ Triumph Trident

The BSA Rocket 3/Triumph Trident is a motorcycle from Triumph Engineering, a British motorcycle manufacturing company. It was manufactured from 1968 to 1975 with a total of 27,480 units produced. It also was considered the last major motorcycle developed by the company before Triumph Engineering was bought by John Bloor. Additionally, this motorcycle was both badged and sold Triumph Trident and BSA Rocket 3.

Buell XB12R

The Buell XB12R is a sport motorcycle built in 2004 by the Buell Motorcycle Company, an American motorcycle manufacturer. Its exhaust is strategically placed on the underside of the motorcycle. It also features an aluminum frame, 14 liters fuel capacity and 155 miles per hour top speed. Additionally, the XB12R is around 1.92 meters in length, 0.77 meters in width, and 0.78 meters in seat height and weighs about 179 kilograms. The available colors for this particular motorcycle include: black, red, gray and amber.

Confederate Wraith

The Confederate Wraith is a beautiful, exotic and surprisingly ride-able bike built by Confederate Motorcycles, an American manufacturer of exotic street motorcycles. This motorcycle was produced from 2007 to 2009 and was designed by JT Nesbitt by pinning paper cutouts together. It has a comfortable padded seat, long tubular handlebar and fuel tank and battery that are placed under the engine. Moreover, the Confederate Wraith also has minimal lighting and has no fenders or a cover placed over a wheel to prevent mud, sand, rocks, or liquids from being thrown into the air by the rotating tire.

Ducati 1098

The Ducati 1098 is a sport bike manufactured by the Italian company Ducati and was designed by Giandrea Fabbro, Ducati's senior designer. It was produced from 2007 to 2009 and comes in three versions: 1098, 1098S, and 1098R. All these versions come in elegant colors of black, yellow, red and the special edition Tricolore which is a combination of the colors of Italy's flag (red, white and green). It also has horizontal headlights and a 173.3 miles per hour top speed. Furthermore, the Ducati 1098 is a highly respectable racing motorcycle that won many championships, including the 2008 British Superbike Championship, the 2009 FIM Superstock 1000 Cup season, the 2011 Macau Grand Prix and 14 championships at the Superbike World Championship.

Ducati 900SS

The Ducati 900SS is a motorcycle from Ducati. It was manufactured from 1991 to 1998. It was considered one of the best street bikes Ducati has ever built because of its unremarkable speed (219.4 km/h top speed). The 900SS also features a triangulated tube frame near the rear wheel, a 17.5 liter fuel capacity and weighs180 kilograms.

Ducati 916

The Ducati 916 is a sport bike manufactured by Ducati. It was produced from 1994 to 1998. It features an underseat exhaust, a tubular steel frame, 257 to 260 km/h top speed and a 0.79 m seat height. Moreover, Ducati 916 also won several races, including: 4 Superbike World Championships, the eight-lap Formula One class, and Battle of the Twins Open class in 1999.

Ducati 999R

The Ducati 999R is a sport motorcycle built by Ducati in 2006. It is an affordable classic motorcycle that features a single steel exhaust, tubular steel frame, a single seat and a 15.5 liter fuel tank. It also weighs around 181 kilograms and has a 0.78 meters seat height.

Ducati Desmosedici RR

This road-legal replica of the Ducati Desmosedici MotoGP racebike was produced from 2007 to 2008, with only 1,500 units available for public purchase. The Ducati Desmosedici RR also features 188 miles per hour speed, 15 liter fuel capacity and 0.83 meter seat height.

Ducati Multistrada

The Ducati Multistrada is a motorcycle manufactured by Ducati. It was first launched in 2003 and is still being produced up until today. Its name, Multistrada, was derived from the Italian words meaning "many roads", referring to its versatility or capability as a general-purpose street motorcycle. The Motor Cycle News also stated that the Multistrada is "a truly versatile motorcycle". However, the downside to this motorcycle is its small tank that can only hold 20 liters of fuel. In the market, the main competitor of the Multistrada is the BMW GS, which is also a versatile motorcycle.

Ducati Scrambler

A Ducati Scrambler is a scrambler motorcycle manufactured by Ducati. A scrambler, or a motocross, is an off-road motorcycle typically used in races with short and closed off-road tracks that feature different obstacles. It was launched in 2014 at the Intermot motorcycle show; however, the sales of Ducati Scrambler in the US didn't begin until 2015. Additionally, the Ducati Scrambler has a small fuel tank that can only hold about 3.6 gallons of fuel. It has long motorcycle forks at the front so riders can make this particular motorcycle jump at high speeds.

Ducati Supermono

The Ducati Supermono is a lightweight racing motorcycle manufactured by Ducati from 1993 to 1995. Its name was derived from the Supermono, a class in European motorcycle road racing. It was also considered one of the most collectable Ducatis because only 65 Supermono units were built throughout its entire 2 years of production. The 121-kilogram Ducati Supermono is capable of reaching 141 miles per hour top speed and producing 61.4 hp power.

Harley Davidson Low Rider

The Harley Davidson Low Rider or the Low Rider FXS 1200 is a 1970s motorcycle built by Harley-Davidson, an American motorcycle manufacturer. Today, it is considered a highly collectable item. It is also very rarely seen in auctions. It has a chrome finish, lowered rear end, a 98 mph top speed and weighs around 220 kg.

Harley Davidson Road King

The Harley-Davidson Road King is a cruiser motorcycle built by Harley Davidson Inc. A cruiser motorcycle is a motorcycle where the driver's feet are placed forward, hands up and the spine upright or slightly leaning back. It was first launched in 1994 and has become a favorite motorcycle by many people. It features a five-gallon fuel tank, floorboards for the driver and the passenger, and a detachable windshield and saddlebags. Since the introduction of the Road King in 1994, not much has changed in the appearance and performance of the motorcycle.

Harley Davidson Softail

The Harley-Davidson Softails are softail motorcycles manufactured by Harley-Davidson, Inc. (an American motorcycle manufacturer) from 1983 up to present. Softails are motorcycles that have a hidden rear suspension system with shock absorbers for comfort. They were designed to look like the bikes of the past and provide comfort due to their rear suspension. This rear suspension has shock absorbers or springs that make driving safe and comfortable by keeping the passengers cut-off from road bumps and vibrations.

Honda 400 Four

The Honda 400 Four is a motorcycle manufactured by Honda. It was produced from 1975 to 1977 and was first introduced at the Cologne motorcycle show. The press and reviewers were impressed by the 400 Four, however, in America it didn't sell well. Honda decided to revise the model by putting higher bars and footpegs set further forward to boost sales. Unfortunately, despite all the efforts, the Kawasaki was still more popular than the expensive Honda 400 Four. This particular model features 103.8 mile per hour top speed, 4.5 liter fuel capacity, and 178 kilograms weight.

Honda Africa Twin

The Honda Africa Twin or the Honda XRV750 is a large dual-sport motorcycle from Honda. It was manufactured from 1989 to 2003 and was based on the NXR-750 motorcycle that won four times in the Paris-Dakar rally. It features a windscreen, twin headlights, a long dual seat and an aluminum covering that protects the bottom part of the engine from flying debris and impact. It also has a 23 liter fuel capacity, 113 miles per hour top speed and 0.86 meters seat height.

Honda CB750

The Honda CB750 is a motorcycle manufactured by Honda. It was produced from 1969 to 2003 and then in 2007. The CB750 promotes a standard upright riding posture. Dating back to 1969, this motorcycle was also often considered the original Universal Japanese Motorcycle. It has received several awards and recognitions including the AMA Motorcycle Hall of Fame Classic Bikes and the Discovery Channel's "Greatest Motorbikes Ever". Furthermore, the CB750 features 125 miles per hour top speed, 19 liter fuel capacity and 0.79 meter seat height.

Honda CBR1100XX Super Blackbird

The Honda CBR1100XX Super Blackbird is a motorcycle manufactured by Honda from 1996 to 2007. Its name, Blackbird, was derived from the aircraft Lockheed SR-71 (also known as Blackbird), which is a speed record holder. The Super Blackbird was designed specifically to compete with the Kawasaki Ninja ZX-11 as the world's fastest production motorcycle or; motorcycle that is produced in great quantity and can be used on public roads. Fortunately, Honda succeeded and was able to beat Kawasaki Ninja ZX-11 with a top speed of 178.5 miles per hour. However, after two years, the Super Blackbird was beaten by Suzuki Hayabusa, that has 194 miles per hour top speed.

Honda CBR900RR

The Honda CBR900RR is a sport bike manufactured by Honda. It was produced from 1992 to 2003 and was also known as Fireblade in other countries. It features an 18-liter fuel tank, 168 to 180 kilogram weight and 0.81-meter seat height. The Honda CBR900RR is available in different color schemes including pure red, pure yellow, pure black, pure silver, white with blue and red, white with black and red, white with violet and yellow, black with silver and red, black with violet and yellow, and black with red.

Honda CR500

The Honda CR500 which was nicknamed "Ping King" is a motorcycle built by Honda and is typically used for long desert races. It was from Honda's CR series and was produced from 1984 to 2001. With its engine capable of reaching 55 hp, it has been considered the most powerful motorcycle Honda has ever produced.

Honda CT90

The Honda CT90 is a small motorcycle produced by Honda. It was manufactured from 1966 to 1979 and was designed for a particular market such as hunters, fishermen, commuters, and outdoorsmen. Due to its small size, it is perfect for use on off-roads and narrow trails. The CT90 is also ideal for climbing and carrying packs and for street roads as well. Additionally, this motorcycle features 55 miles per hour top speed and a weight of 188 lbs.

Honda Motocompo

The Honda Motocompo is a folding scooter manufactured by Honda. It was built from 1981 to 1983, with a total of 53,369 Motocompo units sold. It was introduced by Honda as a "Trunk Bike" or a bike that could fit inside the trunk of cars like Honda Today and Honda City. As a folding scooter, the Motocompo's seat, foot-pegs and handlebars can be folded and tucked into the scooter's rectangular plastic body. It was best known as the bike Natsumi Tsujimoto used on *You're Under Arrest*, a Japanese seinen manga series. Moreover, the Motocompo also features 2.2-liter fuel capacity, 1-liter oil capacity, 42 kilograms weight and 1.19 overall length.

Honda NR

The Honda NR500 is a racing motorcycle built by Honda HRC, a division of the Honda Motor Company. It was produced in 1979 to enter the Grand Prix motorcycle racing. However, the NR500 wasn't able to win the Grand Prix. Because of this, Honda decided to stop the project and developed the NR500 to compete in the 1982 season of the Grand Prix. Despite not winning the Grand Prix, the NR500 was still able to win a few races at the 1981 Laguna Seca and the 1981 Suzuka 200 kilometer race.

Honda NX650 Dominator

The Honda NX650 Dominator is a motorcycle from Honda, a famous Japanese manufacturing company. It was produced from 1988 to 2000. The original 1998 models of this motorcycle could be started both electronically and by kick starting. However, all later models came up with the electric starting method only. The Dominator is known for its capability both on and off the road. It features 16-liter fuel capacity, 154 kilograms weight and 0.87 meters seat height.

Honda Pan European

The Honda ST1300, or the Honda Pan European, is a sport touring motorcycle from Honda. It was first launched in Europe in 2002 as the ST1300 Pan European, while the introduction in North America happened in 2003, with the model marketed as the ST1300. The production of Pan European ended in 2013 as a new model called the CTX1300 was introduced by Honda; the CTX1300 is a cruiser motorcycle version of the Pan European. The Pan European features 29-liter fuel capacity and 0.79-meter seat height.

Honda RC30

The Honda RC30 or the Honda VFR750R is a racing motorcycle built by Honda Racing Corporation (HRC). It has a fully faired or fully covered body and was specially designed for the World Superbike Championship. It was first launched in Japan in 1987 and then in the United States in 1990. The last one hundred RC30 units built in 1990 were for the England market. This particular motorcycle features 18-liter fuel capacity, 180-kilogram weight and 2.05 overall length. Impressively, the Honda RC30 was able to win the 1988 and 1989 Superbike World Championship and the 1989 and 1990 Macau Grand Prix.

Honda RC51

The Honda RC51 a motorcycle manufactured by a Japanese multinational corporation called Honda. It was produced from 2000 to 2006 and was called RVT1000R in the US and VTR1000 in Europe and Australia. This particular motorcycle was specifically built for Honda's racing teams, to be used in the Superbike World Championship. The Honda RC51 has two versions: those models that were built from 2000 to 2001 which are designated as SP1, and those that were produced from 2002 to 2006 which are designated as SP2. Compared to SP1, the SP2 has a more updated fuel injection system, a system that brings the fuel from the fuel tank to the engine. The Honda RC51 features a 164 miles per hour top speed and 4.8 gallon fuel capacity.

Honda Rune

The Honda Rune, or the Valkyrie Rune, is a limited edition cruiser motorcycle model introduced in 2003. With its very distinctive look of chrome and steel finish, it only costs around US$27,000. It is available in three colors: black, dark red metallic and blue metallic. It features a 23-liter fuel capacity and 28.8-inch seat height.

Honda Super Cub

The Honda Super Cub is an underbone motorcycle manufactured by Honda. An underbone motorcycle is a motorcycle that has tube framing covered by plastic or non-structural body panels. The Super Cub was produced from 1958, with around 87 million units built as of 2014. Because of its popularity, the Super Cub was considered one of the most produced motorcycles in history. Moreover, the Super Cub is a lighter motorcycle compared to other models with its 50–90 kilogram weight.

Honda VFR 800

The Honda VFR800 is a sport touring motorcycle from Honda. Being a sport touring motorcycle, it is capable of performing like a sport bike (i.e. excellent speed and acceleration) while providing comfort for the rider and passenger like a touring motorcycle. It started production in 1998 and is still in production. Its most notable feature is its combined braking system (CBS) or linked braking system (LBS). Compared to the usual breaking system of motorcycles where the breaks at the front and rear wheels are separate, the CBS combines both front and rear brakes into one. The Honda VFR800 also features a 20-liter fuel capacity and 31.7 inch seat height.

Indian Chief Dark Horse

The Indian Dark Horse is a variant of the Indian Chief, a cruiser type motorcycle used in competition and in sport riding. The Dark Horse was introduced and manufactured by the Indian Motorcycle Manufacturing Company, a United States Motorcycle Company on 14th of February 2015 and was based on a Chief Classic but painted in black. It features 20.8-liter fuel capacity, 2.63 meters overall length and 341 kilograms weight.

Indian Chief Vintage

The Indian Chief Vintage is another motorcycle that was based on the Indian Chief motorcycle. It has genuine tan-colored leather saddlebags and a windshield. It measures around 103.7 inches in overall length with a 26-inch seat height.

Indian Scout

The Indian Scout is a motorcycle manufactured by the Indian Motocycle Company, an American motorcycle manufacturing company. The first Indian Scouts were produced from 1919 to 1949. The 101 Scout, or the model version built from 1928 to 1931, has been considered the best motorcycle the Indian Motorcycle Company has ever made. In fact, today, the 101 Scout is still being used in the Wall of Death; a carnival sideshow where motorcyclists travel along the vertical wall of a barrel-shaped wooden cylinder and perform different stunts. When Polaris Industries (an American vehicle manufacturer) bought the Indian Motorcycle Company, a new Scout model was introduced in 2015.

Kawasaki Eliminator

The Kawasaki Eliminator is a motorcycle produced by the Japanese company Kawasaki. It was manufactured from 1985 to 2007. It is a successful cruiser type motorcycle that underwent a lot of changes. The most recent change was in 2005 when the Eliminator became available in black. The new Eliminator also had laid-back comfortable seating for two, a larger fuel tank that could hold 3.4 gallons of fuel, a straight exhaust, and a single headlight.

Kawasaki Ninja H2

The Kawasaki Ninja H2 is a sport class motorcycle manufactured by Kawasaki Heavy Industries since 2015. It was from the Kawasaki Ninja sportbike series. Its name was derived from a motorcycle from the 1970s called Kawasaki H2 Mach IV, which was built by Kawasaki, a Japanese company to awaken the "sleeping motorcycle market". It features a top speed of 210 miles per hour and a 17.03-liter fuel capacity. After the introduction of Ninja H2, a street-legal version of the motorcycle called the Street-legal Ninja H2 has also been shown. It has rear-view mirrors and reduced engine power compared to Ninja H2.

Kawasaki Versys 650

The Kawasaki Versys 650, or the KLE650, is a motorcycle manufactured by Kawasaki since 2007. Its name Versys was derived from the words versatile and system. It features a 19-liter fuel capacity, 206-kilogram weight and 0.85 meter seat height. Amazingly, the Versys 650 also received a couple of awards, including the 2008 Motorcycle of the Year Award by Motorcyclist Magazine, 2008 Best in Class "Allrounder class" award by Motor Cycle News, and 2015 Comparison Winner: Kawasaki Versys 650 LT vs. Suzuki V-Strom 650XT by Motorcyclist Magazine.

Kawasaki W800

The Kawasaki W800 is a motorcycle manufactured by Kawasaki. It was first launched in 2011 and is still in production today. It doesn't have a kick-start (a lever that is kicked with one's foot to start the engine). The W800 features a gloss-painted fuel tank, a ribbed seat, and a beautiful W-logo on each side of the tank. Additionally, this particular model has a 14-liter fuel capacity and 0.79-meter seat height.

Kawasaki Z1

The Kawasaki Z1 is a two passenger motorcycle built by Kawasaki. It was manufactured from 1972 to 1975, with an estimated 85,000 units produced. It was built under the project name 'New York Steak'. It features 130–132 miles per hour top speed and 18-liter fuel capacity. Moreover, the Z1 has an overall length of 2.2 meters and weighs around 230 kilograms. Undeniably powerful, the Z1 set the world FIM and AMA record (in 1972) for 24-hour endurance. It was also the winner of Motorcycle News 'Machine of the Year' from 1973 to 1976.

Kawasaki ZX-10 Tomcat

The Kawasaki ZX-10 Tomcat, or the Ninja ZX-10, is another sport motorcycle from Kawasaki Motorcycles. It was manufactured from 1988 to 1990 and was part of Kawasaki's Ninja line. It has a top speed of 165 miles per hour and was considered the fastest production motorcycle in 1988. The ZX-10 Tomcat features a 21-liters fuel capacity, 245-kilograms weight and 0.79-meter height.

Kawasaki ZZR600

The Kawasaki ZZR600 is a sport touring motorcycle. It was manufactured by Kawasaki from 1990 to 2008. The first generation of ZZR600s, which were named D1, had a standard speedometer on the left, signal lights in amber, a fuel gauge and a temperature gauge. There was also storage under the seat for the motorcycle's manual and registration. An additional compartment that could be only be opened by ignition key could be found on the left side of the unit's fairing or shell cover. Moreover, ZZR600 has an 18-liter fuel capacity and 0.78-meter seat height.

KTM 1190 Adventure

The KTM 1190 Adventure is a motorcycle built by KTM, an Austrian manufacturing company. It was manufactured from 2013 to 2016 and was designed as an adventure touring motorcycle, or a motorcycle that can be used in long-range travel both on road and off-road. It also features a 0.89 m seat height, 212 kg weight and 23-liter fuel capacity. Moreover, the KTM 1190 Adventure was built to compete against other street-going motorcycles like the Ducati Multistrada 1200.

KTM 1190 RC8

The KTM 1190 RC8 is a sport bike manufactured by KTM, an Austrian bicycle manufacturer. It is in production since 2008, with the first models considered KTM's first-ever Superbike design. It features a 16.5-liter fuel capacity and a 31.7-inch seat height. Additionally, the KTM RC8 has joined several motorcycle races since it's launching in 2008 and has announced it will race in the RC8. Some of the races it has entered include the 2008 FIM Superstock Championship, the 2009 and 2010 British Superbike Championship and in 2012 the AMA Pro SuperBike Series where it ended the season in 11th place overall.

KTM 950 Adventure

The KTM 950 Adventure is a dual-sport motorcycle manufactured by KTM, an Austrian bicycle manufacturer. It was produced from 2003 to 2005 and underwent a couple of modifications. It has an engine that reaches around 102 bhp and 215 km/h top speed. It is available in different colors including grey-black, black, orange and blue-orange. The 950 Adventure also features 22-liter fuel capacity, 3.3-liter oil capacity, tubular steel frame, and weighs around 206 kilograms.

Laverda Jota

The Laverda Jota was a motorcycle built by Laverda, an Italian manufacturer of high performance motorcycles. It was built from 1976 to 1982. Its engine can reach 90 hp and more than 140 mph speed. It has also been considered one of the fastest production motorcycles or a mass-produced motorcycle that can be used on public roads. The Laverda Jota also features a 20-liter fuel capacity and 238 kilogram weight.

Metisse Desert Racer

The Metisse Desert Racer or Steve McQueen Desert Racer is a motorcycle built by Metisse Motorcycles, a British motorcycle manufacturer in cooperation with Steve McQueen's estate. It is an exact replica of the motorcycle that Bud Etkins and Steve McQueen (a famous American actor) built together to join a desert race in 1966. There are only 300 replicas built and each cost around US$19,836. The Desert Racer features 5 piece body panels in grey gel coat, a Metisse logo with Steve McQueen's autograph on the fuel tank and an 8-liter capacity fuel tank. It is also available in a dual seat option with matching foot pegs. The measurements of the Desert Racers are as follows: length - 2 m, width - 0.90 m, and height – 1.15 m.

Moto Guzzi Le Mans

The Moto Guzzi Le Mans is a sports motorcycle that was first launched in 1976 by Italian company Moto Guzzi. Its name was derived from an endurance race held in France called the 24 Hours of Le Mans. When it comes to racing, the Le Mans finished 4th in the 24-hour race at Barcelona's Montjuïc circuit and has won in the 1977 Britain's Avon Production Machine championship. It also had race success multiple times at the AMA Superbike Championship in the US.

Moto Guzzi V7 Racer

The Moto Guzzi V7 Racer is another motorcycle from Moto Guzzi. It is an undeniably out-of-the-box racer with its dropped handle-bars, chrome finished tank, upswept pipes, and beautiful red tubular frame. Aside from its stunning look, the V7 Racer is also easy to ride and has an impressive 115 miles per hour top speed.

Moto Guzzi V8

The Moto Guzzi V8 is a motorcycle manufactured by Moto Guzzi and designed by Giulio Cesare Carcano. It was also known as the Otto motorcycle and was specifically developed to enter the 1955 to 1957 season of the Moto Guzzi Grand Prix. With its unique appearance, it has been ranked by the Discovery Channel as one of the ten greatest motorbikes of all time. This particular model also features an engine that can reach 78 hp and 171 mph top speed.

MTT Y2K Turbine Motorcycle

The MTT Y2K Turbine Motorcycle is a motorcycle built by Marine Turbine Technologies (MTT), a US turbine manufacturer. It was manufactured from 2000 to 2005 and was only made to order for buyers with a long term warranty. Unlike other motorcycles, the Y2K is powered by diesel, kerosene and Bio-Fuel. It is considered the fourth greatest motorcycle by the Discovery Channel. It is also a Guinness World Record holder for being the world's fastest production motorcycle and for being the most expensive one at a cost of around US$150,000. Moreover, the Y2K features a turboshaft engine, 34-liter fuel capacity and 0.84 meter seat height.

Norton 961 Commando

The Norton 961 Commando is a motorcycle built by Norton Motorcycles, a company from Oregon that bought the rights to the Norton brand name. It was manufactured in 2006 and was based on the original Norton Commando motorcycle. However, due to a lack of funding, the 961 Commando never reached production in America. Luckily, a UK businessman named Stuart Garner acquired the Norton brand and re-launched newer versions of the 961 Commando. These new versions have a 17.03-liter fuel capacity, 188-kilogram weight and 0.81 seat height.

Norton Commando

The Norton Commando is a motorcycle produced by the Norton Motorcycle Company, a British motorcycle manufacturing company. It was built from 1967 to 1977, during which time it became popular all over the world. One of the proofs of the Norton Commando's remarkable success is the "Machine of the Year" award it received for five successive years (1968-19720). The award was given by the Motor Cycle News (MCN); a UK weekly motorcycling newspaper. Moreover, the Norton Commando also has a 10-liter fuel capacity, 115 miles per hour top speed, 33 – 34 inch seat height and 190 kilogram weight.

Norton Jubilee

The Norton Jubilee is a motorcycle built by Norton, a British motorcycle manufacturing company. It was manufactured from 1958 to 1966 and was named to honor Norton's Diamond Jubilee of 60 years of motorcycle manufacture. It has a very small engine; the smallest one Norton has ever made with its 60mm x 44mm dimensions. It can also only produce 12 kW of power and is about 150 kg in weight.

Norton Manx

The Norton Manx is a racing motorcycle manufactured by Norton Motors Ltd. It was produced from 1947 to 1962 and was specifically developed to win the Isle of Man TT. The development of this motorcycle was delayed due to World Word II but it appeared for the 1946 Manx Grand Prix. In fact, its name 'Manx' was derived from 'Manx Grand Prix', motorcycle races held on the Isle of the Man TT Course. Depending on the size, the Manx can reach 115, 130 or 140 miles per hour top speed.

Royal Enfield Continental GT

A Royal Enfield Continental GT is a café racer, or a lightweight motorcycle, typically used for quick travel over short distances. It was manufactured by Royal Enfield, an Indian motorcycle manufacturing company, and was considered the company's lightest, fastest, most powerful motorcycle. The Continental GT is also an ideal café racer that allows body positioning pushed forward with high knees. This position makes the driver hug the tank. The Continental GT has a 13.5-liter fuel capacity, 184 kilogram weight and 2.06 meter overall length with 0.80 meters seat height.

Saietta R

The Saietta R is an electric motorcycle produced by the British company Agility. It has been available commercially since 2013 and costs around $35,000. It has a powerful motor that can run for 112 miles and can reach 80 miles per hour top speed. It features a low handlebar, long seat and rear-set footpegs.

Suzuki 600 Bandit

The Suzuki 600 Bandit is a motorcycle produced by Suzuki Motor Corporation, a Japanese multinational corporation. This particular model is from Suzuki's Bandit Series. The Bandit Series is a series of standard or general purpose motorcycles. The 600 Bandit in particular was manufactured from 1995 to 2003. It is a best-seller model of Bandit and was named as one of the best motorcycles for all types of riders due to its versatility on the road. The 600 Bandit also features a 0.80 meter seat height, an 18-liter fuel capacity, 129 miles per hour top speed and steel tube frame.

Suzuki Biplane

The Suzuki Biplane is a concept motorcycle; a motorcycle that has been shown in motorcycle shows with possible intent to enter production at a future date. Concept motorcycles are like samples created to get customer's reaction or opinion. The Suzuki Biplane in particular was unveiled by Suzuki at the 2007 Tokyo Auto Show where it has been on display until today. Its design was inspired by the Wright Flyer biplane built by the Wright brothers. In fact, it has colors similar to the canvas usually used on older aircraft. It also doesn't have any wind protection, leaving the rider exposed to the elements, just like a pilot of an open-top aircraft.

Suzuki Boulevard C50

The Boulevard C50 is a cruiser style motorcycle built by Suzuki Motor Corporation. It was from the Suzuki Boulevard range of motorcycles. The C50, in particular, has been built from 2005 up to the present. Before 2005, this motorcycle was launched as the Volusia in 2001 at the Daytona Bike Week. However, when 2005 came, Suzuki re-branded the model as the Suzuki Boulevard C50. This motorcycle measures around 98.4 inches in length and about 27.6 inches in seat height. The C50 also features a 16-liter fuel capacity and 45.1 hp engine power.

Suzuki Boulevard M50

The Boulevard M50 (Intruder M800 outside North America) is another cruiser motorcycle from the Suzuki Boulevard range of motorcycles. It was manufactured by Suzuki from 2005 up to present. This motorcycle features a black painted engine and mag wheels, LED taillight and 15.5 liter fuel capacity. Additionally, the M50 measures around 0.70 meters in seat height, 2.4 meters in overall length and 0.89 meters in width. Unfortunately, the M50 didn't sell very well so after 5 model years Suzuki did a complete makeover of the model.

Suzuki GSX-R 750

The Suzuki GSX-R750 or 'Gixxer' is a sports motorcycle manufactured by Suzuki since 1985. This particular motorcycle was from Suzuki's GSX-R series. In appearance, it is somewhat similar to a Suzuki Endurance, a racing motorcycle. The only difference is that the GSX-750 is affordable and is perfect for road use as it is equipped with side mirrors.

Suzuki Hayabusa

The Suzuki Hayabusa is a sport motorcycle manufactured by Suzuki. It started production in 1999 and is considered one of the world's fastest production motorcycles with its 188 to 194 miles per hour top speed. Aside from its speed, the Hayabusa is also noted for its all-round performance; it is easy to handle, comfortable to ride on, reliable and comes with a reasonable price tag. Indeed, this particular model is a successful one with sales growing in number every year since its introduction in 1999. As of June 2007, more than 100,000 Hayabusa units were sold all over the world.

Suzuki Intruder

The Suzuki Intruder is a series of cruiser motorcycles from Suzuki. Its production started in 1985 and began in North America with the Intruder 700 and the Intruder 1400 models. Throughout their entire production life, the Intruders have undergone several changes. However, in 2005 Suzuki decided to make dramatic changes with the Intruder and rename it 'Boulevard'.

Suzuki RG500 Gamma

The Suzuki RG500 Gamma is a sport motorcycle manufactured by Suzuki. It was produced from 1985 to 1987, with a total of 9,284 units built. In Asia, this particular motorcycle is available as RG400. In total, there were about 6,213 RG400 units completed. Furthermore, the RG500 is about 2.10 meters in length, 0.70 meters in width and 0.77 meters in seat height. It also has a 22 L fuel capacity, a 236.4 km/h top speed and weighs around 154 kg.

Suzuki SV650

The Suzuki SV650 is an internationally available motorcycle typically used on the streets. It was manufactured by Suzuki from 1999 to 2012 and was replaced by SFV650 Gladius. However, when the Gladius name was discontinued in 2016, the SV650 came back. The SV650 is available in the following generations: first generation (1999-2002), second generation (2003-2012) and third generation (2016). All these generations differ slightly in their appearance and performance.

Suzuki V Storm 650

The Suzuki V-Strom 650 or the DL650 (in Europe, Oceania and the Americas) is a touring motorcycle manufactured by Suzuki. It was first introduced in 2004 and still remains in production until today. It features a standard or upright riding posture, a 22-liter fuel capacity and 220-kilogram weight. The V-Strom 650 is also quite popular worldwide because of its capability to be used in different riding conditions like commuting, touring, cruising or even off-roading. Additionally, in 2007, the Motorcyclist, a USA magazine, considered the V-Strom 650 one of the "ten best" bikes under $10,000.

Triumph Bonneville

The Triumph Bonneville is a standard motorcycle manufactured first by Triumph Engineering and then by Triumph Motorcycles Ltd, which are both British motorcycle manufacturers. It was produced in the following generations: 1959–1983, 1985–1988 and 2001–present. The first two generations were made by Triumph Engineering while the third was built by Triumph Motorcycles. This last generation was actually a new design that strongly resembled the first two series. All these generations are similar in appearance and only differ in engine power. Its name, Bonneville, was derived from Bonneville Salt Flats in Utah, USA where Triumph and others attempted to top the motorcycle speed records.

Triumph Model H

The Triumph Model H or the 'Type H' or 'the Trusty' is a motorcycle that looks like a regular bicycle. It was manufactured by Triumph Engineering Co Ltd. from 1915 to 1923 with about 57,000 units built. It was the first Triumph machine that had no pedals (like what bicycles have), hence, considered a true motorcycle. The Model H is also a reliable motorcycle during wartime despite its weak front fork, which can break on rough ground.

Triumph Speed Triple

The Triumph Speed Triple is a motorcycle built by Triumph Motorcycles, the largest British motorcycle manufacturer. It has been produced from 1994 up to the present and is considered one of the earliest motorcycles with a streetfighter style. The streetfighter style has no fairing, a large shell that covers the engine of the motorcycle. It is also characterized by having a pair of round headlights, upright handlebars and short but loud exhaust. The Triumph Speed Triple motorcycle also has a 15.5-liter fuel capacity and 0.83-meter seat height.

Triumph Thruxton

The Triumph Thruxton is a series of motorcycles manufactured by Triumph Engineering and then by Triumph Motorcycles. It was originally launched in 1965 as a limited edition café racer or a lightweight motorcycle typically used for quick rides over short distances. However, in 2004 a modern version of the Thruxton was introduced. This version features rear set footrests, reverse-cone exhaust silencers and 16-liter fuel capacity.

Triumph Tiger 900

The Triumph Tiger 900 is a motorcycle manufactured by the largest British motorcycle manufacturer, Triumph Motorcycles Ltd. It was produced from 1993 to 1998 and was also known as the 'Steamer'. In the UK, where it was made, this particular sport motorcycle only sold small numbers of units. However, in other countries like USA and Germany, this dual sport motorcycle was successful. It has a 0.25-liter fuel capacity, weighs 209 kilograms and has a 0.85 m seat height that allows the driver of the motorcycle to see over traffic.

Triumph X75 Hurricane

The Triumph X-75 Hurricane was originally destined to be the BSA Rocket3. However, after the BSA factory closed in 1972, this motorcycle was revived in 1973 as the Triumph X75 Hurricane. It features glass fiber bodywork, a fuel tank that can carry 3 gallons of fuel and three exhausts. It is also being considered as the model that creates the 'cruiser class' of motorcycles. Cruisers are motorcycles that feature a certain riding posture where the rider's feet are usually positioned forward, the hands up and the back in an upright position or leaning back slightly.

Velocette Venom

The Velocette Venom is a British motorcycle manufactured by the motorcycle manufacturer Veloce Ltd. It was produced from 1955 to 1970 with around 5,721 built in total. With its 100.05 miles per hour top speed, a Velocette Venom set the 24-hour world record in 1961 at a racetrack in France called Montlhéry. Amazingly, it was the first motorcycle of its size to achieve such speed for 24 hours. In fact, as of 2008, no motorcycle of the same capacity was able to equal this record.

Vincent Black Shadow

The Vincent Black Shadow is a hand-built motorcycle by Vincent HRD, a British manufacturer of motorcycles. It was specifically built as a response to a demand for a more "sports oriented model". Since its introduction in 1948, the Black Shadow became very popular for its distinctive predominantly black color that is unusual but stunning. Sixteen "White Shadows" were also built which was made from Black Shadow's specification but with plain aluminum finish. It has an overall weight of about 208 kg. In total, there are a little less than 1,700 Vincent Black Shadows produced and all of these were hand-assembled.

Yamaha FS1-E

The Yamaha FS1-E is a small motorcycle manufactured by Yamaha. It was manufactured in the 1970s. It was especially designed for the European market and has been registered in the UK since August 1978 with a restricted 31 miles per hour maximum. Furthermore, the FS1-E also has a 6.5-liter fuel capacity, 1.78 meters overall length, 0.56 meter width and 0.94 meter height.

Yamaha FZR600

Yamaha FZR600 was a sports motorcycle manufactured by Yamaha. It was produced from 1989 to 1999. It had a steel frame, 18-liter fuel capacity and 3.1-liter oil capacity. It is also about 2.10 meters in length, 0.70 meters in width, 0.785 meters in seat height and weighs around 181 kilograms. The FZR600 is considered, by many, one of the best sports motorcycles and is a popular choice for many amateur racers. Aside from being attractive, it is also fast and inexpensive. Despite being popular, the production of FZR600 was stopped to make way for the YZF-R6, another sports motorcycle from Yamaha.

Yamaha GTS 1000

The Yamaha GTS1000 is a sport-touring motorcycle by Yamaha. It was produced from 1993 to 1996. It is best noted for its forkless front suspension or the lack of fork-like structure that connects the front wheel to the front end of the vehicle. Instead, it has a special front suspension that connects the front wheel to the lower part of the vehicle. This suspension adds an additional cost that consumers didn't find reasonable, so the GTS1000 was not commercially successful. This motorcycle had 31.1 inch seat height, 553 pound weight and 5.3-gallon fuel capacity.

Yamaha RD350LC

The Yamaha RD350LC is a motorcycle manufactured by Yamaha. It was built for three years, from 1980 to 1983. Throughout its production years, it underwent some changes. During its final production, it was manufactured in Brazil as the RD350R. Originally, the RD350LC was designed for the European market, where it became an instant hit. In fact, Yamaha sold over 10,000 units in Europe in the first 9 months of production. The RD350LC features 16-liter fuel capacity and 154-kilogram weight.

Yamaha Road Star

The Yamaha Road Star, or Yamaha XV1600A, is a cruiser-style motorcycle built by Yamaha starting 1999. Up until today, this particular motorcycle is still being produced and has undergone a few minor changes. This model is very popular among custom bike builders as it's easy to customize. In line with this customization, the Road Star comes with a Silverado or Midnight package that includes: a back rest, studded saddle bags, studded driver and passenger seats, and a windscreen. For a couple of years a so-called "S" package also became available and included more chrome pieces for the buyer. Additionally, the Road Star features a 20-liter fuel capacity and 0.71-meter seat height.

Yamaha SDR 200

The Yamaha SDR200 is another motorcycle from Yamaha. It was manufactured from 1986 to 1987. Originally, it was intended for the Japanese market only, however, some units were taken out of the country as grey imports. Grey imports are new or used motorcycles legally imported from another country. The most notable characteristic of a Yamaha SDR200 is its small size: 1.95 m length, 0.68 m width and 0.77 m seat height. It also only weighs around 105 kg and holds about 9.5 L of fuel.

Yamaha Thundercat

The Yamaha Thundercat, or the Yamaha YZF600R, is a sports bike manufactured by Yamaha. It was produced from 1996 to 2007. It is considered as a sport touring motorcycle: a motorcycle that is capable of high-performance just like a sport bike and can also be used for long-distance traveling that provides comfort just like a touring motorcycle. The Thundercat also features a length of 2.06 m, width of 0.72 m, seat height of 0.81 m and 19 L fuel capacity.

Yamaha Virago 535

The Yamaha Virago 535 is a cruiser-style motorcycle from Yamaha Motor Corporation and was manufactured from 1987 to 2003. It has a distinctive heavily chromed body styling and was quite small compared to other cruising motorcycles. It featured an 8.6 or 13.5-liter fuel capacity and 2.8-liter oil capacity. When the Virago 535 was discontinued in 2004 in the US and 2003 in the UK, the "star" range became the newest cruiser line from Yamaha.

Yamaha XT500

The Yamaha XT500 is a motorcycle manufactured by Yamaha, a Japanese motorcycle manufacturer. It was produced from 1975 to 1981. This motorcycle can be used off-road and in enduro, an off-road motorcycle race that features different challenges and obstacles. Additionally, it can also be used on streets and can be registered and licensed. As compared to other sports bikes, Yamaha XT500 is equipped with street-legal equipment like mirrors, lights, speedometer, horn, muffler or silencer and a mounting place for a license plate. Due to these features, the Yamaha XT500 became an instant success after its launch in the US in 1975 and in Europe in 1976. Additionally, it also won the first big African rallies (a long distance off-road racing that takes place over several days).

Yamaha YZF R1

The Yamaha YZF-R1 or Yamaha R1 is a sport bike built by Yamaha. It was produced since 1998 up to present. It is also considered one of the greatest motorcycles ever created by Yamaha. In fact, the R1 had 5 wins in the Macau Grand Prix. It also won in the 2004 and 2005 FIM Superstock 1000 Cup, in the 2009 Superbike World Championship, in the 2015 Suzuka 8 Hours endurance race and in the 2015 British Superbike series title. The YZF-R1, depending on the model, has 17 or 18-liter fuel capacity and 168–182 miles per hour top speed.

Yamaha YZF-R7

The Yamaha YZF-R7 was a race motorcycle manufactured by Yamaha in 1999. It was a limited edition motorcycle and only 500 units were produced. It was specifically developed to join the Superbike World Championship and the Suzuka 8 Hour endurance races. It is about 2.06 meters in length, 0.72 meters in width and has 0.84 meter seat height. The YZF-R7 also weighs around 176 kilograms and has 23-liter fuel capacity.

Other amazing picture books by Melissa Ackerman for young kids to enjoy

Butterflies for Kids

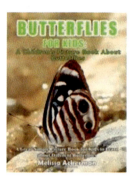

Spiders for Kids

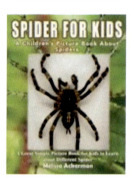

Animals in Africa

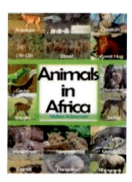

If you like what you've read or want to share how this book has help your child's learning, please leave a review here. It will be greatly appreciated!!!

Images From: bluXgraphics(motorcycle design Japan)=Midorikawa, Marcela Escandell, Steven Tyler PJs, John Y. Can, Epic Fireworks, Burt, Pete Coleman, zenithe, Craig Howell, Gregory Mathieu, Bill Abbott, RAVDesigns, Ronald Saunders, Thomas Altfather Good, kazamatsuri, Daniel Hartwig, Brian Snelson, Klaus Nahr, Michele Testini, Davide Restivo, Werner Bayer, Martin Burrow, alijava, emperornie, Vir Nakai, GorissenM, David, Toby Charlton-Taylor, cosmoflash, H-Y-P-E, Gunner111, F. D. Richards, gnustang, Iwao, Flattrackers and Caferacers Parts and bikebuilds, gronman www.gronmanphotos.com, Johnnie B, Carlos Enrique Gil Carrillo, Steve Parker, Mike Oliveri, Chad Horwedel, Bob Adams, Dave Thompson, 威翰 陳, Robert Tadlock, Armin Vogel, JUN 4 1 4, big-ashb, Jason O'Donnell, Iain Farrell, Alexey Vinokurov, Mitchell McPherson, Tony Hisgett, big-ashb, Hiroshi Miyazaki, Bryn Pinzgauer, Tristan Nitot, Aneo, Keith, dazfuller, Steve Glover, tomislav medak, D.Fletcher, cdemo, Mark, zenith, pixelfever, Stefan Jürgensen, RL GNZLZ, Greg Goebel, Wolftrouble, StooMathiesen, SoulRider.222, Eddy Clio, jambox998, Roderick, Masatoshi Nishinaga, Tamas, r reeve, PSParrot, /Flickr